THIS WALKER BOOK BELONGS TO:

_____

_____

_____

_____

For

Atha Tehon

First published 1996 in Great Britain by
Walker Books Ltd
87 Vauxhall Walk
London SE11 5HJ

This edition published 1997

First published 1995 by
Dial Books for Young Readers, New York

2 4 6 8 10 9 7 5 3 1

This book has been typeset in Cochin.

Printed in Hong Kong

British Library Cataloguing in Publication Data
A catalogue record for this book is
available from the British Library.

ISBN 0-7445-5260-5

EDWARD'S
FIRST NIGHT AWAY

ROSEMARY WELLS

WALKER BOOKS
AND SUBSIDIARIES
LONDON • BOSTON • SYDNEY

The telephone rang. It interrupted
Edward's story. "I'm sure he'd love to
come," said Edward's mum.

"Won't it be fun to play in the snow at Anthony's house!" said Edward's dad.

"When will you come back for me?"
asked Edward.
"Soon," answered his mum and dad.

Anthony's mother welcomed
everyone into the kitchen.

"Promise you will come back soon?"
asked Edward.
"We promise!" said his mum and dad.

Edward and Anthony made a
snowman. Snow began to fall.

Soon it was snowing so hard, they
could not see. "Cocoa time!" called
Anthony's mother.

The telephone rang. It was Edward's
mum. "The snow is too deep to come
and fetch you," she said.

"You'll have to spend the night at Anthony's. Be brave, my little sausage!"

"Would you like to play with
my train?" asked Anthony.
"No," said Edward.

"Would you like a biscuit?"
asked Anthony.
"No, thank you," said Edward.

Edward did not eat supper.
His mum and dad called to say
goodnight.

"Now you feel better!" said
Anthony's dad.
But Edward did not feel better.

Edward could not sleep, even in
Anthony's new pyjamas.

Anthony's mother and father couldn't
bear watching.

So Anthony's mother dug a path
to the car.

Anthony's father lay under the car
and put snow chains on the tyres.

They followed the snowplough all the
way to Edward's house.

"He wasn't quite ready to stay overnight," said Anthony's father.

"But he *is* ready for cinnamon toast,"
said Edward's mum.

During Edward's bedtime story the
telephone rang.

But this time,
no one answered it.

MORE WALKER PAPERBACKS
For You to Enjoy

Some more Edward the Unready books by Rosemary Wells

EDWARD'S FIRST DAY AT SCHOOL

When Edward goes to playschool, he isn't *quite* ready
to join in with the other children.

0-7445-5259-1   £4.50

EDWARD'S FIRST SWIMMING PARTY

When Edward goes to Georgina's birthday party at the
swimming pool, he isn't *quite* ready to
give up his water wings!

0-7445-5261-3   £4.50

Walker Paperbacks are available from most booksellers, or by post from B.B.C.S., P.O. Box 941, Hull, North Humberside HU1 3YQ

24 hour telephone credit card line 01482 224626

To order, send: Title, author, ISBN number and price for each book ordered, your full name and address,
cheque or postal order payable to BBCS for the total amount and allow the following for postage and packing:
UK and BFPO: £1.00 for the first book, and 50p for each additional book to a maximum of £3.50.
Overseas and Eire: £2.00 for the first book, £1.00 for the second and 50p for each additional book.

Prices and availability are subject to change without notice.